CLASSICS Illustrated ®

Mary Shelley
FRANKENSTEIN

essay by
Debra Doyle, Ph.D.

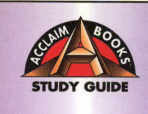

ACCLAIM BOOKS
STUDY GUIDE

Frankenstein
Originally published as Classics Illustrated no. 26

Art by Hayward Webb and Ann Brewster
Adaption by Ruth A. Roche
Cover by Jordan Raskin

For Classics Illustrated Study Guides
computer recoloring by Colorgraphix
editor: Madeleine Robins
assistant editor: Gregg Sanderson
design: Joseph Caponsacco

Dale-Chall R.L.: 7.85

ISBN 1-57840-044-9

Acclaim Books, New York, NY
Printed in the United States

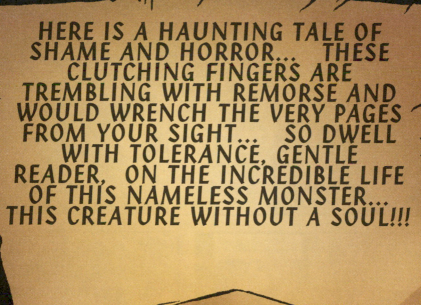

HERE IS A HAUNTING TALE OF SHAME AND HORROR... THESE CLUTCHING FINGERS ARE TREMBLING WITH REMORSE AND WOULD WRENCH THE VERY PAGES FROM YOUR SIGHT... SO DWELL WITH TOLERANCE, GENTLE READER, ON THE INCREDIBLE LIFE OF THIS NAMELESS MONSTER... THIS CREATURE WITHOUT A SOUL!!!

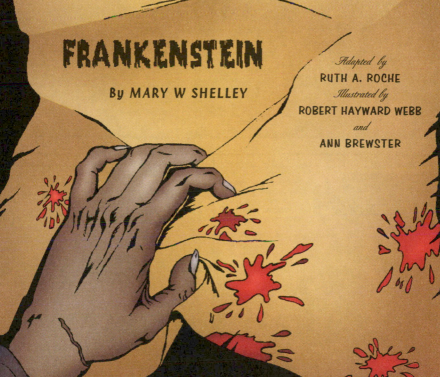

FRANKENSTEIN

By MARY W SHELLEY

Adapted by
RUTH A. ROCHE
Illustrated by
ROBERT HAYWARD WEBB
and
ANN BREWSTER

YOU MUSTN'T PULL ON THE LOCKET, DEAREST, IT WILL BREAK, AND IT CONTAINS A PICTURE OF YOUR LOVELY MOTHER!

BUT IT'S SO PRETTY, AREN'T YOU MY MOTHER, ELIZABETH?

ELIZABETH IS YOUR COUSIN, WILLIE. HAVEN'T WE EXPLAINED THAT TO YOU BEFORE?

BUT I REMEMBER WHEN MOTHER DIED, FATHER! I EVEN REMEMBER WHEN ELIZABETH CAME TO LIVE WITH US.

OUR STORY UNFOLDS AT A GAY FAMILY OUTING ATTENDED BY THOSE WHOM FATE HAS ALREADY MARKED FOR DEATH... NEVER APPREHENDING, THEY ARE HAPPY - SEEKING NO MORE THAN THE SMALL PLEASURES OF A PICNIC...

YOU HAVE A GOOD MEMORY, ERNEST, CONSIDERING THAT YOU WERE SUCH A CHILD WHEN IT ALL HAPPENED.

HEY! HELLO YOUNG MAN!

HENRY!

IF VICTOR WON'T PLAY WITH YOU, HENRY, I WILL. YOU NAME THE GAME.

I DIDN'T EXACTLY ASK HIM TO PLAY, WILLIE, HE'S VERY BUSY WITH HIS CHEMISTRY, BUT AS FOR US... HOW ABOUT HIDE AND SEEK, EH!

BUT SUDDENLY...

RAIN! OH DEAR, SPOILING OUR LOVELY HOLIDAY! HURRY, EVERYBODY, IT WILL SOON BE COMING DOWN IN TORRENTS!

VICTOR WON'T BE DISAPPOINTED! HE LOVES STORMS, DON'T YOU, SON?

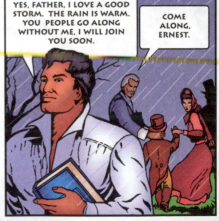

YES, FATHER, I LOVE A GOOD STORM. THE RAIN IS WARM. YOU PEOPLE GO ALONG WITHOUT ME, I WILL JOIN YOU SOON.

COME ALONG, ERNEST.

HOW WELL I RECALL FATHER EXPLAINING THE ELEMENTS OF ELECTRICITY TO ME WHEN I WAS A CHILD. ITS POWER FOR DESTRUCTION FILLS ME WITH AWE.

TO THINK THAT TOMORROW I SHALL BE LEAVING ALL THIS AND ACTUALLY GETTING TO SCHOOL. IT SHOULD SADDEN ME TO LEAVE MY FAMILY. YET I CANNOT BUT REJOICE AT THE OPPORTUNITY OF BEING ABLE TO WORK IN A UNIVERSITY LABORATORY.

OH, VICTOR! YOU'LL CATCH COLD.

DON'T WORRY ABOUT ME, DEAR GIRL. I'LL SOON GET DRY...

SON, YOU'VE GOT TO THINK OF OTHER THINGS BESIDES THE WONDERS OF STEAM AND ELECTRICITY. SCIENCE HAS ITS PLACE, BUT A MAN MUST THINK OF A WIFE, TOO, YOU KNOW!

UNTIL I SATISFY MY THIRST FOR KNOWLEDGE IN CHEMISTRY, I SHALL FEEL UNWORTHY OF ELIZABETH. SHE UNDERSTANDS.

IT WAS HIS MOTHER'S DYING WISH THAT WE SOMEDAY WED, AND I KNOW HE WON'T FORGET THE VOW HE MADE TO HER. YET HE TARRIES SO...

COME. YOU'D BETTER RETIRE, SON. IT'S A LONG WAY TO INGOLSTADT. YOU'LL WANT TO BE FRESH IN BODY AND SPIRIT FOR THE JOURNEY.

I SHALL MISS YOU, FATHER. SOMETIMES I REGRET THE URGE OF SCIENCE THAT REGULATES MY FATE AND TAKES ME FROM MY FAMILY.

THE NEXT MORNING.

GOD - SPEED, SON. WE'LL LOOK FORWARD TO YOUR LETTERS. DO NOT FORGET US.

I'LL WRITE REGULARLY, FATHER. GOODBYE, BOYS! GOODBYE ELIZABETH!

I SHALL MISS YOU, VICTOR.

WHAT CAN I SAY TO YOU, ELIZABETH? FIND COMFORT WITH MY PEOPLE WHO LOVE YOU SO WELL AND I PROMISE MY RETURN SHALL BE SOONER THAN YOU EXPECT.

GOODBYE, SON!

FAREWELL, VICTOR!

GOODBYE, VICTOR, GOODBYE!

DON'T GRIEVE, ELIZABETH. I HAVE A PLEASANT SURPRISE FOR YOU. I HAVE EMPLOYED LITTLE JUSTINE MORITZ TO HELP YOU WITH THE YOUNGSTERS. IT WILL ALLOW YOU MORE LEISURE... SAY, TO WRITE TO VICTOR.

DEAR UNCLE, I HAVE ALWAYS LOVED JUSTINE.

SUDDENLY A FAMILIAR FIGURE APPEARS ON THE ROAD.

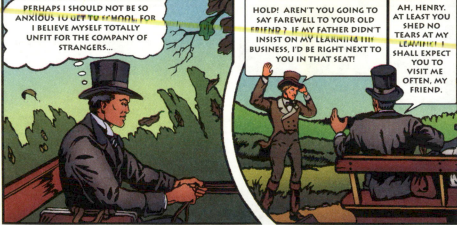

PERHAPS I SHOULD NOT BE SO ANXIOUS TO GET TO SCHOOL, FOR I BELIEVE MYSELF TOTALLY UNFIT FOR THE COMPANY OF STRANGERS...

HOLD! AREN'T YOU GOING TO SAY FAREWELL TO YOUR OLD FRIEND? IF MY FATHER DIDN'T INSIST ON MY LEARNING THE BUSINESS, I'D BE RIGHT NEXT TO YOU IN THAT SEAT!

AH, HENRY. AT LEAST YOU SHED NO TEARS AT MY LEAVING! I SHALL EXPECT YOU TO VISIT ME OFTEN, MY FRIEND.

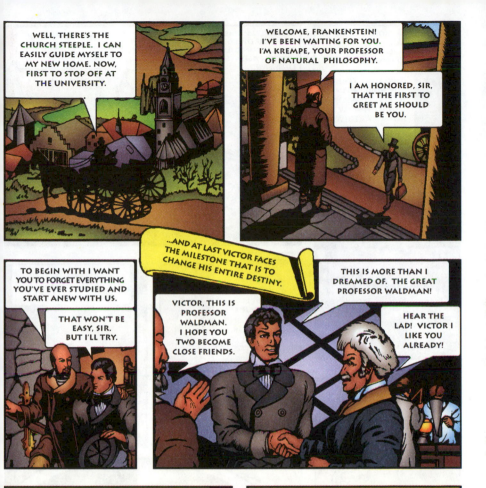

WELL, THERE'S THE CHURCH STEEPLE. I CAN EASILY GUIDE MYSELF TO MY NEW HOME. NOW, FIRST TO STOP OFF AT THE UNIVERSITY.

WELCOME, FRANKENSTEIN! I'VE BEEN WAITING FOR YOU. I'M KREMPE, YOUR PROFESSOR OF NATURAL PHILOSOPHY.

I AM HONORED, SIR, THAT THE FIRST TO GREET ME SHOULD BE YOU.

...AND AT LAST VICTOR FACES THE MILESTONE THAT IS TO CHANGE HIS ENTIRE DESTINY.

TO BEGIN WITH I WANT YOU TO FORGET EVERYTHING YOU'VE EVER STUDIED AND START ANEW WITH US.

THAT WON'T BE EASY, SIR. BUT I'LL TRY.

VICTOR, THIS IS PROFESSOR WALDMAN. I HOPE YOU TWO BECOME CLOSE FRIENDS.

THIS IS MORE THAN I DREAMED OF. THE GREAT PROFESSOR WALDMAN!

HEAR THE LAD! VICTOR I LIKE YOU ALREADY!

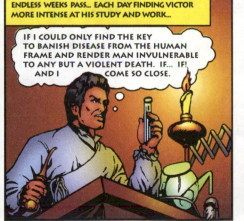

ENDLESS WEEKS PASS... EACH DAY FINDING VICTOR MORE INTENSE AT HIS STUDY AND WORK...

IF I COULD ONLY FIND THE KEY TO BANISH DISEASE FROM THE HUMAN FRAME AND RENDER MAN INVULNERABLE TO ANY BUT A VIOLENT DEATH. IF... IF! AND I COME SO CLOSE.

ONLY UTTER EXHAUSTION CAUSES HIM TO PAUSE IN THE SECRET EXPERIMENT AND SEEK REST IN HIS PRIVATE CHAMBER.

DEAR ELIZABETH, SUCH A FAITHFUL CORRESPONDENT! IF SHE ONLY KNEW HOW REMOTE THEY ALL SEEM TO ME. I'M GLAD JUSTINE MAKES HER SO HAPPY. I MUST FIND TIME TO WRITE. IT'S BEEN SO LONG...

MONTH UPON MONTH ROLLS ON AND IT IS AGAIN NOVEMBER... DISMAL, DESOLATE, NOVEMBER.

TWO LONG YEARS OF WORKING IN SECRET... TONIGHT SHALL FINALLY SHOW MY RESULTS. SUCCESS OR FAILURE! IT'S NOW UP TO FATE AND THIS LAST INJECTION!

SUDDENLY... SLOWLY... THE INANIMATE CREATURE OPENS ITS DULL YELLOW EYES... A CONVULSIVE MOTION AGITATES ITS LIMBS AND... IT BREATHES...

SAINTED MOTHER! WHAT HAVE I CREATED? IT... IT'S A DEMON!

WHAT FOOL DREAMS LED ME ON... THIS MONSTER IS CONCEIVED THROUGH MADNESS... I CAN'T BEAR TO LOOK AT IT...

SLEEP... I MUST SLEEP... CAN'T THINK OF WHAT TO DO NEXT...

RRSSPPSSTT...

GET AWAY FROM ME, FIEND! DON'T TOUCH ME!

I'M LOSING MY MIND. MUST GET AWAY... MUST...

WILL HE FOLLOW ME? I PRAY TO HEAVEN HE WON'T DARE.

MORNING, DR. FRANKENSTEIN, WHAT BRINGS YOU ABOUT SO EARLY? ARE YOU COMING IN OR GOING OUT?

HMM... ALWAYS TOLD MY WIFE HE WAS A STRANGE ONE.

WHAT SHALL I DO?

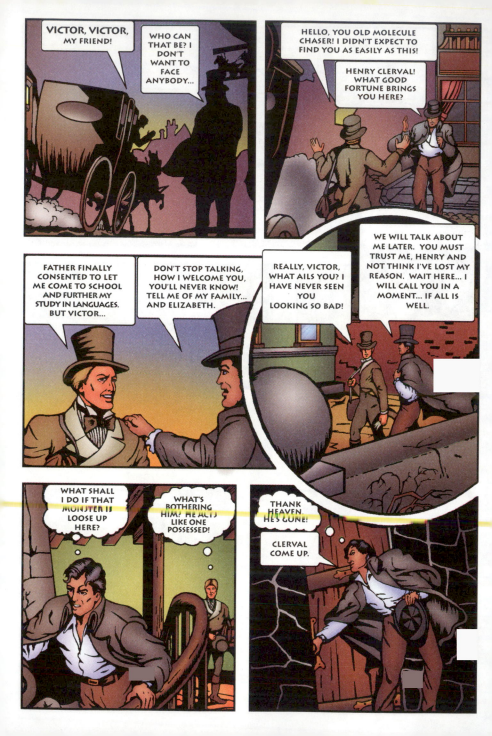

VICTOR, I DEMAND YOU TELL ME WHAT HAS COME OVER YOU. I AM YOUR FRIEND. HAVE YOU BEEN WORKING TOO HARD?

TOO HARD? THAT'S A FINE JOKE! HA, HA, HA...

WORKING TOO HARD! WHAT A FINE JOKE... HA, HA, HA...

VICTOR... VICTOR!

HOUSEKEEPER! RUN AND FETCH PROFESSOR WALDMAN. QUICKLY! DOCTOR FRANKENSTEIN HAS FAINTED!

TENSE MOMENTS LATER...

NERVOUS FEVER. HE'LL RECOVER, BUT HE MUST RESTRAIN HIMSELF FROM WORKING SO HARD ON HIS SECRET EXPERIMENTS!

SHHH... DON'T MENTION HIS WORK, PROFESSOR, THAT'S WHAT SEEMED TO SEND HIM OFF. I'LL SEE THAT HE REMAINS QUIET.

I'M SURE HE'S IN GOOD HANDS. YOU'RE A TRUE FRIEND, CLERVAL. KEEP IN TOUCH WITH ME.

THANK YOU, PROFESSOR.

SECRET EXPERIMENT, EH! I THOUGHT SO... WELL, HE'LL TELL ME ABOUT IT IN DUE TIME.

SLOWLY, THE WEEKS PASS...

WHERE HAVE YOU BEEN ALL MORNING? AHH.. HENRY... HOW CAN I EVER REPAY YOU FOR ALL YOU'VE DONE FOR ME?

NONSENSE! LOOK, I'VE BEEN AFTER THE MAIL... HERE'S A LETTER FROM HOME. THEY KNOW NOTHING OF YOUR ILLNESS, SO IT SHOULD BE CHEERFUL NEWS !

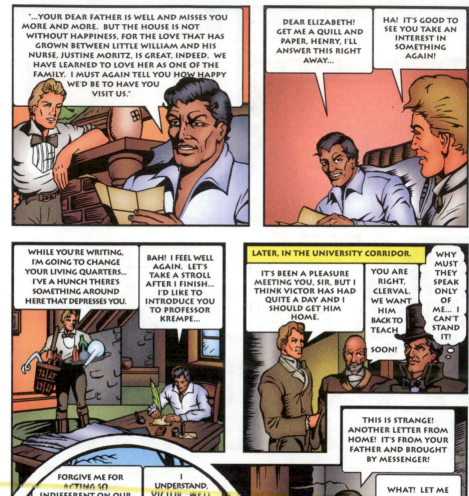

"...YOUR DEAR FATHER IS WELL AND MISSES YOU MORE AND MORE. BUT THE HOUSE IS NOT WITHOUT HAPPINESS, FOR THE LOVE THAT HAS GROWN BETWEEN LITTLE WILLIAM AND HIS NURSE, JUSTINE MORITZ, IS GREAT, INDEED. WE HAVE LEARNED TO LOVE HER AS ONE OF THE FAMILY. I MUST AGAIN TELL YOU HOW HAPPY WE'D BE TO HAVE YOU VISIT US."

DEAR ELIZABETH! GET ME A QUILL AND PAPER, HENRY, I'LL ANSWER THIS RIGHT AWAY...

HA! IT'S GOOD TO SEE YOU TAKE AN INTEREST IN SOMETHING AGAIN!

WHILE YOU'RE WRITING, I'M GOING TO CHANGE YOUR LIVING QUARTERS... I'VE A HUNCH THERE'S SOMETHING AROUND HERE THAT DEPRESSES YOU.

BAH! I FEEL WELL AGAIN. LET'S TAKE A STROLL AFTER I FINISH... I'D LIKE TO INTRODUCE YOU TO PROFESSOR KREMPE...

LATER, IN THE UNIVERSITY CORRIDOR.

IT'S BEEN A PLEASURE MEETING YOU, SIR, BUT I THINK VICTOR HAS HAD QUITE A DAY AND I SHOULD GET HIM HOME.

YOU ARE RIGHT, CLERVAL. WE WANT HIM BACK TO TEACH SOON!

WHY MUST THEY SPEAK ONLY OF ME... I CAN'T STAND IT!

FORGIVE ME FOR ACTING SO INDIFFERENT ON OUR VISIT... PERHAPS I DID TOO MUCH TODAY...

I UNDERSTAND, VICTOR. WE'LL SOON BE HOME AND YOU CAN REST.

THIS IS STRANGE! ANOTHER LETTER FROM HOME! IT'S FROM YOUR FATHER AND BROUGHT BY MESSENGER!

WHAT! LET ME TAKE A LOOK AT IT, HENRY!

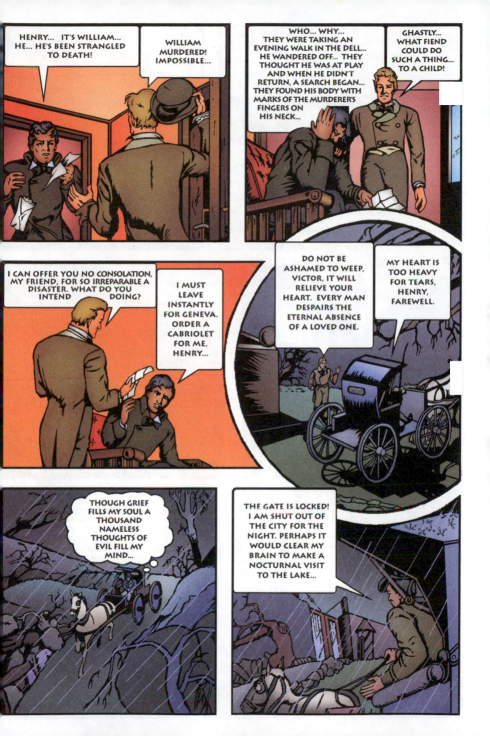

MR. VICTOR! IT'S YOU...

SHHH, DON'T AWAKEN THE FAMILY, I WILL SEE THEM IN THE MORNING. THEY NEED THEIR SLEEP AFTER WHAT THEY'VE BEEN THROUGH...

THIS HOUSE WILL NEVER BE THE SAME WITHOUT YOU, LITTLE BROTHER. MY SOUL IS IN ANGUISH, A THOUSAND DEVILS TORTURE IT...

SUDDENLY, ERNEST ENTERS THE ROOM... TWO YEARS HAVE MADE A GREAT CHANGE IN THE YOUTH.

WELCOME, VICTOR. IT IS AN UNHAPPY WELCOME... WITH THE SHADOW OF DEATH HOVERING OVER THIS HOUSE.

ERNEST! HOW YOU'VE GROWN! THE OTHERS, HOW ARE THEY?

ELIZABETH REQUIRES CONSOLATION. SHE FELT IT WAS HER FAULT SINCE WILLIAM HAS BEEN HER WARD ALL THESE YEARS. I NEED NOT TELL YOU OF FATHER, BUT SINCE THE MURDERER HAS BEEN DISCOVERED...

DISCOVERED! BUT WHO COULD OVERTAKE HIM?

I DON'T KNOW WHAT YOU MEAN, VICTOR! IT WAS A GREAT SHOCK TO US THAT JUSTINE COULD BE SO LOVING TO WILLIAM AND AT THE SAME TIME BE SO WICKED,

JUSTINE MORITZ MURDERED WILLIAM?!

CIRCUMSTANCES PROVED IT! THE MORNING AFTER THE MURDER SHE SUDDENLY TOOK TO HER BED AND WENT INTO A STRANGE SLUMBER! IN HER POCKET A SERVANT CHANCED TO SEE THE LOCKET ELIZABETH HAD PUT ON WILLIAM'S NECK BEFORE HIS DEATH! TO THINK A LOCKET WAS TEMPTATION FOR MURDER!

NO... NO! IT'S A MISTAKE!

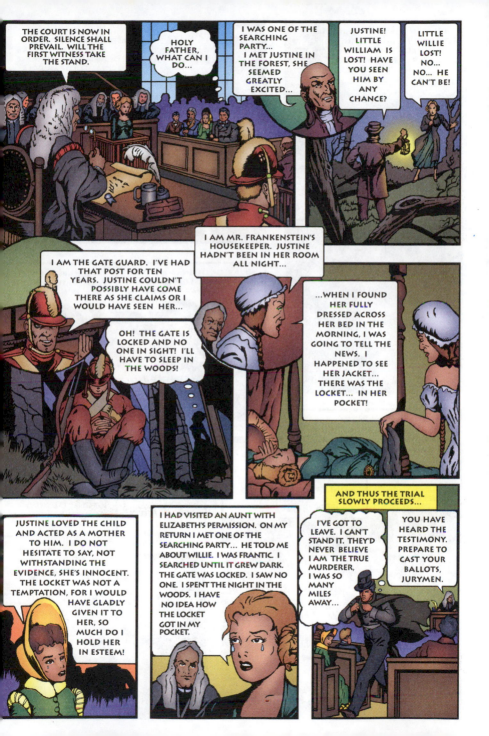

HOW CAN THEY CONDEMN THIS YOUNG GIRL FOR THE CRIME COMMITTED BY A MONSTER OF MY CREATION, YET WHO WILL BELIEVE ME... WHAT SHALL I DO?

WELL? GUILTY?

OH, VICTOR, YOU LEFT BEFORE YOU SAW WHAT HAPPENED! JUSTINE BROKE DOWN AND CONFESSED! SHE DID COMMIT THE MURDER! OH... VICTOR...

ELIZABETH, LISTEN TO ME. IT ISN'T TRUE. WE MUST GET TO HER AND FIND OUT WHAT MADE HER SAY SUCH A THING!

PERHAPS THEY WILL LET US SEE THE GIRL IN HER CELL.

BY SPECIAL PERMISSION THEY ARE GRANTED AN AUDIENCE WITH THE DOOMED MAID...

JUSTINE! WHAT MADE YOU CONFESS TO A CRIME WE KNOW YOU DIDN'T COMMIT?

I GREW SO WEARY OF ALL THEIR CONFUSING QUESTIONS... YET NOW I'M TRULY MISERABLE. FOR I CONFESSED A LIE, BUT IT IS TOO LATE TO TRY TO TAKE IT BACK

SOON I WILL JOIN MY SWEET WILLIAM. THAT ALONE CONSOLES ME.

JUSTINE. I'LL THINK OF SOMETHING. DEPEND ON IT!

TIME TO LEAVE.

OH, VICTOR!

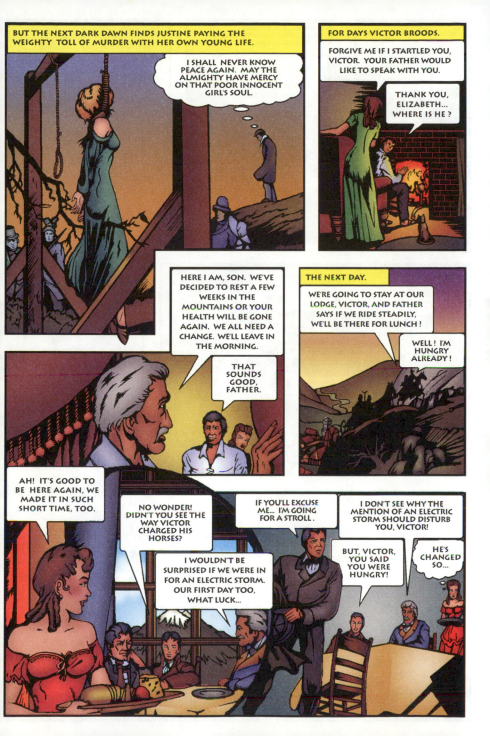

WILLIAM... JUSTINE... I'M TWICE A MURDERER. WHAT RIGHT HAVE I TO LIVE... I FEEL NOTHING BUT SHAME AND LOATHING FOR MYSELF...

SUDDENLY, A SOUND... THE CRUNCH OF A HEAVY TREAD, GROWING IN MOMENTUM...

WHAT'S THIS? AH! THAT SHADOW! SO! OUR PATHS CROSS AGAIN! THIS TIME I'LL KILL HIM.

ABHORRED MONSTER! THE TORTURES OF HADES ARE TOO MILD A VENGEANCE FOR YOUR CRIMES...

BE CALM, I ENTREAT YOU. HEAR ME. I, TOO, HAVE SUFFERED.

YOU SPEAK! HATED DEVIL, SO YOU'VE LEARNED TO USE YOUR TONGUE!

YES, IT IS TRUE. I AM HATED AND DO SPEAK. YOU MUST LISTEN TO ME.

COME. FOLLOW ME TO MY CAVE.

SPEAK, THEN! AND WHILE YOU TALK, I WILL FIGURE OUT A WAY TO KILL YOU!

BEGONE! THERE CAN BE NO COMMUNION BETWEEN US. WE ARE ENEMIES. BEGONE, OR MATCH STRENGTH IN A BOUT THAT WILL DOOM ONE OF US!

BELIEVE ME, VICTOR FRANKENSTEIN, I COULD KILL YOU WITH A SINGLE BLOW! BUT YOU ARE MY CREATOR AND THAT MUST NOT BE. HEAR ME OUT...

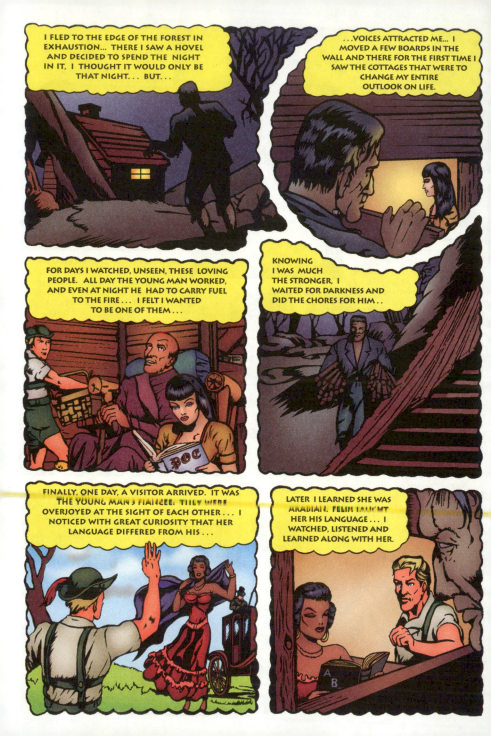

WHILE PASSING THROUGH THE FOREST, I MET WITH PICNICKERS. THEY WERE HAVING GREAT SPORT. MY HEART ACHED THAT I COULD NOT BE HAPPY AS THEY WERE... WHEN SUDDENLY...

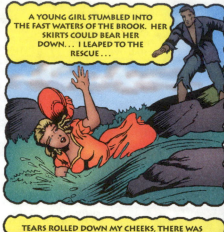

A YOUNG GIRL STUMBLED INTO THE FAST WATERS OF THE BROOK. HER SKIRTS COULD BEAR HER DOWN... I LEAPED TO THE RESCUE...

HER COMPANION DIDN'T UNDERSTAND... HE SHOT AT ME. I DROPPED THE GIRL AND RAN OFF... BLOOD AND PAIN RACKED MY SHOULDER... I CURSED THE BITTER FATE THAT MADE ME SUCH A MONSTER THAT ALL SHUNNED AND EVEN TRIED TO KILL....

TEARS ROLLED DOWN MY CHEEKS, THERE WAS NOT A LIVING THING I COULD CALL FRIEND... BUT...

A LITTLE CHILD APPEARED, HE DIDN'T FEAR ME LIKE THE OTHERS...

I DECIDED TO TAKE HIM WITH ME AND TEACH HIM TO BE MY FRIEND. EVERY MAN NEEDS A FRIEND...

NO! NO! PUT ME DOWN!

HUSH, LITTLE MAN. I WON'T HURT YOU...

I REFUSE! NO TORTURE SHALL EVER EXTORT ME TO DO SUCH A THING! NEVER!

I DO NOT THREATEN YOU, CREATOR, I REASON WITH YOU. GIVE ME A WIFE FOR A FRIEND AND I PROMISE TO QUIT EUROPE FOREVER. I'LL DEPART FOR SOME REMOTE LAND AND LIVE THE REST OF MY DAYS IN QUIET.

GRANT ME THIS WISH, CREATOR. I DESERVE SOME CHANCE FOR HAPPINESS, ALL MEN EXPECT THAT OF LIFE.

YOU MAKE A DEVIL'S BARGAIN, BUT IF I THOUGHT YOU WOULD CLEAR OUT OF EUROPE FOREVER IT WOULD BE WORTH IT TO ME.

I HAVE NO NEED TO SHAKE YOUR HAND. I WILL CREATE YOU A WIFE AND I HAVE WAYS TO SEE THAT YOU KEEP YOUR PROMISE.

I SHALL NOT TROUBLE YOU OR YOURS AGAIN. BUT I WILL BE BY YOUR SIDE, ALWAYS. THIS IS ONE BARGAIN YOU CANNOT BREAK. VICTOR FRANKENSTEIN.

VICTOR RETURNS WITH A STRANGE ELATION FLARING IN HIS HEART...

VICTOR! WE'VE BEEN FRANTIC WITH FEAR OVER YOU!

NONSENSE, FATHER. I'M FEELING BETTER THAN I HAVE IN MONTHS!

AFTER TWO RESTFUL WEEKS... THE RETURN TO GENEVA...

WELL, SON, YOU SEEM TO BE FEELING SO MUCH BETTER... I WANT TO REMIND YOU AGAIN OF ELIZABETH... YOU HAVE KEPT THE POOR GIRL WAITING...

I HAVE THOUGHT OF THAT, FATHER. I MUST GO TO ENGLAND FOR A WHILE... THEN... IF SHE'LL HAVE ME...

LATER, VICTOR SEIZES AN OPPORTUNITY TO SPEAK TO ELIZABETH...

YOU HAVE BEEN SO PATIENT... WILL YOU WAIT JUST TWO MORE YEARS? I'M CERTAIN TO BE MY OLD SELF THEN. IT'S SOMETHING I CAN'T EXPLAIN NOW, DEAREST. YOU MUST HAVE FAITH IN ME.

OH, VICTOR! I BEG YOU TO TAKE CARE OF YOURSELF. AND YOU KNOW IN YOUR HEART, I'LL WAIT!

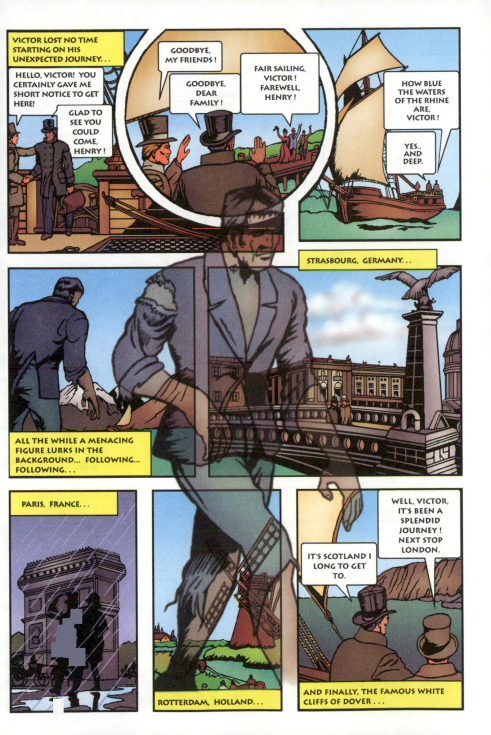

THE TIME PASSES QUICKLY AND SOON TWO TRAVELERS ARE STANDING ON SCOTTISH SOIL...

JUST LOOK AT THE PERTH LANDSCAPE, HENRY! IT'S MORE BEAUTIFUL THAN I EXPECTED!

YES, BUT WE'VE WALKED MILES, VICTOR. LET'S REST IN THE NEXT VILLAGE PUB.

AH! THIS IS MORE LIKE IT! PHEW! I'M TIRED!

MAY I RELIEVE YOU OF YOUR BAG, SIR?

THANK YOU, BUT I PREFER HAVING IT WITH ME.

I CAN'T UNDERSTAND YOUR NOT WANTING TO PART WITH THAT, VICTOR, IT'S BEEN WITH YOU SINCE WE LEFT HOME!

THEN I FEAR THERE IS SOMETHING ELSE YOU WON'T UNDERSTAND, HENRY.

DON'T BE OFFENDED, BUT I'M LEAVING YOU IN PERTH. I'VE RENTED A DESERTED HUT IN THE ORKNEYS TO DO A LITTLE RESEARCH.

AS YOU WISH, MY FRIEND.

AND SO, ABRUPTLY AND WITHOUT EXPLANATION, VICTOR PARTS WITH HIS FOND COMPANION... SETTING OUT ACROSS THE MOORS, ALONE...

WELL, VICTOR FRANKENSTEIN, WHO KNOWS WHAT THIS SECOND EXPERIMENT WILL RESULT IN...

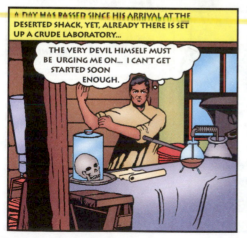

A DAY HAS PASSED SINCE HIS ARRIVAL AT THE DESERTED SHACK, YET, ALREADY THERE IS SET UP A CRUDE LABORATORY...

THE VERY DEVIL HIMSELF MUST BE URGING ME ON... I CAN'T GET STARTED SOON ENOUGH.

THAT NIGHT, TIRED AND WROUGHT, VICTOR SEEKS RELAXATION AND SOLACE ON A WINDSWEPT BEACH... IN THE BACKGROUND A FAMILIAR FIGURE WAITS... WATCHES...

PERHAPS IT IS WRONG WHAT I DO... BUT I HAVE GONE TOO FAR... I MUST SEE IT THROUGH...

FIEND! CREATOR OF DEMONS, YOU HAVE BROKEN YOUR PROMISE!

TRUE, BUT YOU MAY HAVE YOUR REVENGE, MONSTER. KILL ME! I WILL NOT STRUGGLE AGAINST YOU.

WHAT KIND OF JUSTICE WOULD YOU CALL THAT? EVEN AN OUTCAST CREATURE LIKE MYSELF CAN THINK OF BETTER. I GO NOW, VICTOR FRANKENSTEIN, BUT I SHALL RETURN ON YOUR WEDDING NIGHT AND THEN SEEK MY REVENGE!

FLAMES RAGE THROUGH THE HOUSE OF DOOM, LIGHTING THE BEACH WHERE VICTOR FLEES TO HIS FRAIL CRAFT...

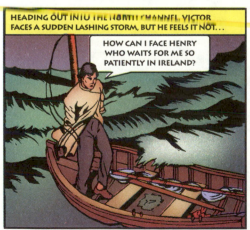

HEADING OUT INTO THE NORTH CHANNEL, VICTOR FACES A SUDDEN LASHING STORM, BUT HE FEELS IT NOT...

HOW CAN I FACE HENRY WHO WAITS FOR ME SO PATIENTLY IN IRELAND?

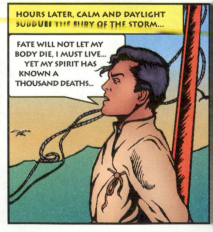

HOURS LATER, CALM AND DAYLIGHT SUBDUE THE FURY OF THE STORM...

FATE WILL NOT LET MY BODY DIE, I MUST LIVE... YET MY SPIRIT HAS KNOWN A THOUSAND DEATHS...

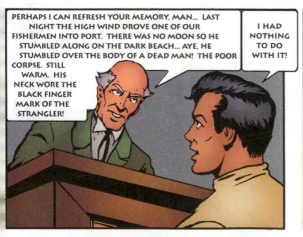

SO YOU DO KNOW HIM, EH?

HENRY! HENRY CLERVAL! MY FRIEND!

FRIEND, HE CALLS HIM!

HAVE MY MURDEROUS MACHINATIONS DEPRIVED YOU OF LIFE ALSO, DEAREST FRIEND?! THO I HAVE ALREADY DESTROYED... OTHER VICTIMS MAY AWAIT THE SAME DESTINY! BUT YOU... MY FRIEND...

KINDLY HAVE HIM REVIVED IN A CELL. HE'S A SICK MAN, PATRICK.

SURE, AND THAT IT SEEMS, MR. KIRWIN!

NO LONGER ABLE TO SUPPORT THE AGONIZING MENTAL TORTURE, VICTOR LAY AT THE POINT OF DEATH FOR TWO LONG MONTHS... BUT HE WAS DOOMED TO LIVE... A KINDLY NURSE TENDS HIM...

NURSE... NURSE.

THERE NOW! DON'T WASTE YOUR STRENGTH TELLING ME AGAIN THAT YOU'RE INNOCENT. I'M YOUR FRIEND. I BELIEVE YOU!

VICTOR, MY BOY, I'M PLEASED TO SEE YOU LOOKING STRONGER. I HAVE HEARD FROM YOUR FATHER AGAIN!

PLEASE GO AWAY, MR. KIRWIN, I CAN'T BEAR TO HEAR MY FATHER'S NAME MENTIONED IN THIS PLACE...

HE IS HERE VICTOR!

NO, NO! TAKE HIM AWAY... FOR MERCY'S SAKE, DO NOT LET HIM ENTER...

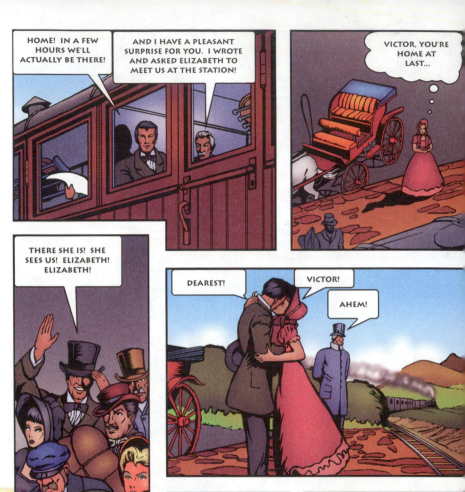

SOON AFTER, ELIZABETH AND VICTOR WERE MARRIED....
A STRANGE COUPLE, HAPPY YET SOMEHOW QUIET...
AS IF A GREAT FEAR POSSESSED THEM...

SUCH A BEAUTIFUL BRIDE!

ELIZABETH MY WIFE...

VICTOR, I'M SO HAPPY...

VICTOR! PUT ME DOWN, YOU SILLY BOY!

TO THE LODGE. THAT'S FAR ENOUGH FROM EVERYONE!

STEALING AWAY FROM THE WEDDING GUESTS, THEY DRIVE TO THE SECLUDED LODGE TO BE ALONE... BUT A CHILL OF UNSEEN TERROR FILLS VICTOR'S HEART...

ELIZABETH! YOU'RE TREMBLING... AFRAID OF THIS DARKNESS?

NONSENSE, VICTOR! IT WILL BE ENTIRELY DIFFERENT ON THE INSIDE WHEN WE LIGHT THE CANDLES!

EVEN AT THIS MOMENT, THE WORDS OF THE MONSTER RING IN VICTOR'S EARS. "I SHALL RETURN ON YOUR WEDDING NIGHT, THEN SEEK MY REVENGE."

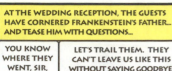

AT THE WEDDING RECEPTION, THE GUESTS HAVE CORNERED FRANKENSTEIN'S FATHER... AND TEASE HIM WITH QUESTIONS...

YOU KNOW WHERE THEY WENT, SIR, TELL US!

LET'S TRAIL THEM. THEY CAN'T LEAVE US LIKE THIS WITHOUT SAYING GOODBYE!

WHAT TRICKS ARE YOU UP TO?

MEANWHILE...

THERE! THAT'S MUCH BETTER!

I WON'T LET ANYTHING HAPPEN... I WON'T... I WON'T!

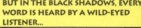

VICTOR!

DON'T BE STARTLED, BELOVED... WHILE YOU GO TO YOUR ROOM, I WANT TO MAKE CERTAIN THAT EVERY DOOR IS SAFELY LOCKED FOR THE NIGHT.

BUT IN THE BLACK SHADOWS, EVERY WORD IS HEARD BY A WILD-EYED LISTENER...

YOU WILL SOON FIND OUT, VICTOR FRANKENSTEIN, THAT UNLIKE YOU... I KEEP MY PROMISES.

LOOK! LIGHTS IN THE LODGE! JUST AS WE SUSPECTED... WILL THEY BE SURPRISED TO SEE US!

ALAS! WHAT IS THIS DREADFUL APPREHENSION I FEEL, CLOUDING THE HAPPIEST DAY OF MY LIFE...

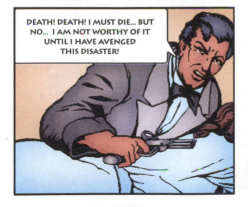

MILES AHEAD OF VICTOR, RELENTLESSLY LEADING ON, THE MONSTER PRESSES THROUGH A RAGING, HOWLING BLIZZARD. . .

WHAT IS THIS? HOWLING DOGS! LUCK IS WITH ME! SOME POOR DEVIL HAS KNOWN DEATH FROM THE COLD, BUT I CAN MAKE GOOD USE OF HIS DOGS AND SLED!

MUSH, MY FOUR LEGGED FRIENDS, FOR FRANKENSTEIN WILL SOON BE UPON US, BARING HIS WRATH UPON MY HEAD. I WANT TO GIVE HIM A GOODLY CHASE FIRST. . .

I SEE HIM! I'VE GOT YOU NOW, MONSTER... I'VE GOT YOU NOW!

THE ICE... CRACKING! IN THE NAME OF THE HEAVENLY FATHER, WHY MUST THIS HAPPEN TO ME NOW?

WHAT SHALL I DO... ONLY TWO DOGS LEFT. . .

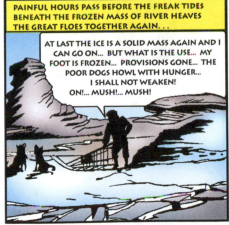

PAINFUL HOURS PASS BEFORE THE FREAK TIDES BENEATH THE FROZEN MASS OF RIVER HEAVES THE GREAT FLOES TOGETHER AGAIN. . .

AT LAST THE ICE IS A SOLID MASS AGAIN AND I CAN GO ON... BUT WHAT IS THE USE... MY FOOT IS FROZEN... PROVISIONS GONE... THE POOR DOGS HOWL WITH HUNGER... I SHALL NOT WEAKEN! ON!... MUSH!... MUSH!

OTHER HEARTS KNOW THE TERROR OF THE ICE... THE CREW ABOARD A THREE MASTED SCHOONER HAVE BEEN CAUGHT IN THE JAM FOR DAYS...

LOOKS LIKE WE'LL BE SPENDING THE REST OF OUR LIVES LOCKED IN THE ICE HERE AT ARCHANGEL...

NOT NECESSARILY, MATE. SOMETHING MAY HAPPEN, THE ICE HAS BEEN RUMBLING FOR DAYS... SAY! WHAT'S THAT?

TWO MEN!

IT'S A GIANT! A DEMON! HE'LL CURSE OUR SHIP! KILL HIM!

THE GIANT'S DISAPPEARED INTO THIN AIR! BUT LOOK! THE OTHER HAS TUMBLED!

HE SEEMS INJURED! WE'D BEST RESCUE HIM!

CAREFUL, LADS, HE STILL LIVES!

AYE! AND THAT'S A MIRACLE...

COME NOW, MAN, JUST SIP THIS...

TELL THE FIRST MATE TO COME HERE IMMEDIATELY!

AYE, AYE. SIR.

HE'S A GONER ALL RIGHT.

THEN WE MUST GET HIS STORY FOR THE LOG, BEFORE IT'S TOO LATE.

CAN YOU HEAR ME, MATE? TRY TO SPEAK. WE MAY YET BE ABLE TO HELP YOU.

HE'S MOVING HIS LIPS! HE'S TRYING TO TALK.

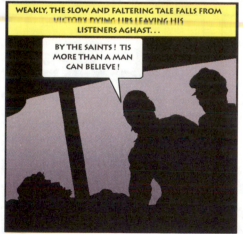

WEAKLY, THE SLOW AND FALTERING TALE FALLS FROM VICTOR'S DYING LIPS LEAVING HIS LISTENERS AGHAST...

BY THE SAINTS! TIS MORE THAN A MAN CAN BELIEVE!

HE'S FINISHED, POOR DEVIL

AYE. MAY PEACE BE WITH HIS TORMENTED SOUL.

FRANKENSTEIN

MARY SHELLEY

"It lives!"

Mary Shelley, in her introduction to the 1831 edition of *Frankenstein; or, The Modern Prometheus*, describes her inspiration for the initial image of her story in these words:

> *I placed my head on my pillow, I did not sleep, nor could I be said to think. My imagination unbidden, possessed and guided me.... I saw with shut eyes, but acute mental vision, —the pale student of unhallowed arts kneeling beside the thing he had put together, I saw the hideous phantasm of a man stretched out, and then, on the working of some powerful engine, show signs of life and stir with an uneasy, half vital motion. Frightful must it be; for supremely frightful would be the effect of any human endeavor to mock the stupendous mechanism of the Creator of the world. His success would terrify the artist; he would rush away from his odious handywork, horror stricken....He sleeps; but he is awakened; he opens his eyes; behold, the horrid thing stands at his bedside, opening his curtains and looking on him with yellow, watery, but speculative eyes.*

Readers wondered at the time how a young woman—not much more than a girl, really, since she was only nineteen when she began writing the story—could come up with such striking and horrific images. Some of the answers may lie in the author's own early life, and others in the peculiar circumstances surrounding the writing of the novel's first draft… because Mary Shelley was a long way from being a well-behaved Regency miss.

THE AUTHOR

Mary Shelley's mother was Mary Wollstonecraft—a pioneer feminist, the author of *A Vindication of the Rights of Woman*, and an observer of the early days of the French revolution. Mary Wollstonecraft had her first child, Fanny, out of wedlock by a lover, Gilbert Imlay. The relationship failed, and Mary Wollstonecraft later married the English philosopher William Godwin. She died on September 10, 1797, from complications after the birth on August 30 of her second daughter, young Mary. William Godwin married again, to a woman named Jane Clairmont. His new wife had a daughter, also named Jane (later she called herself "Clare"), who thus became Mary's step-sister.

Young Mary and her stepmother didn't get along, and eventually William Godwin sent Mary to live with friends in Scotland, where she was educated. She came home in 1812, at the age of sixteen. "After this my life became busier," she says in her introduction to the 1831 edition, and it certainly did.

At her father's house she met a young man, the poet Percy Bysshe Shelley. Shelley's wife Harriet (who had herself been sixteen at the time of her marriage to Shelley) was with him at the time of the visit; nevertheless, Mary and Percy fell in love.

Later Shelley wrote to a friend about his first marriage, "I felt as if a dead and living body had been linked together in loathsome and horrible communion." He hadn't felt this way, apparently, when he eloped to Scotland with Harriet in 1811, but things change.

Divorce, in early 19th century England, was nearly impossible. Those who desired freedom from unsuitable or no longer pleasing mates had to take more direct action. In 1814, two years after their first meeting, Percy Shelley and the not-quite-eighteen-year-old Mary Godwin ran off together, taking Mary's step-sister, Clare (*nee* Jane) Clairmont, with them. William Godwin cut off relations with Mary after the elopement; nevertheless, he continued to give Shelley money for them to live on.

The family—now living in Europe—needed it. Mary's first child was born in March of 1815 and died a few days later. Her second, William Shelley, was born on January 24, 1816, less than six months before she began writing *Frankenstein*. Also in 1816, Percy Shelley's abandoned wife, Harriet, committed suicide. She died on the 7th of December; Percy and Mary were married on December 30th, only 23 days after her death.

In 1818, the Shelleys settled in Italy, where Percy wrote some of his most famous poetry (including "Prometheus Unbound") and Mary continued to write novels and verse dramas. Their friends in Italy included the essayist and critic Leigh Hunt and his family. But Mary's life was not an easy one; during her years with Shelley, she bore five children, of whom only one, named Percy after his father, survived to adulthood. In the summer of 1822, a few days before his 30th birthday, Percy was drowned while attempting to sail from Leghorn to Le Spezia, Italy. His body washed ashore ten days later, and Mary Shelley was a widow at the age of 25.

After Percy's death, Mary Shelley returned to England with her one surviving child, young Percy, and continued to write. The remainder of her life was spent writing biographies, short stories, and four more novels. One of her later novels, *The Last Man* (1826), is set in the 21st century and deals with war, plague, and human extinction. She never remarried. In 1851, Mary Shelley succumbed to a brain tumor and died, with her son and daughter-in-law by her side.

By the time Mary Shelley wrote the preface to the 1831 edition of *Frankenstein*, she had put the wild days of her early life far behind her. Her description of the origin of the novel is sedate—almost staid—considering the book itself, and its turbulent beginning:

In the summer of 1816, we visited Switzerland and became the neighbours of Lord Byron.... But it proved a wet, uncongenial summer, and incessant rain often confined us for days to the house. Some volumes of ghost stories, translated from the German into French, fell into our hands.... 'We shall each write a ghost story,' said Lord Byron; and his proposition was acceded to.

Serious Romantics

With her husband Percy, Mary Shelley was a figure at the heart of the English Romantic movement. In the Enlightenment movement of the 18th century, reason, scientific inquiry and logic ruled. In contrast, the Romantics who followed them (the movement lasted roughly from 1750-1870) believed in passion, in the value of their own feelings and subjective experience, in imagination rather than reason, emotion over logic. If form (in literature, in art, even in music) got in the way of passion and spontaneity, then form took a back seat.

Given Mary's family and education it was perhaps inevitable that she'd be a part of the group of writers and artists who celebrated the spontaneous, the passionate, and the "natural." Her father, William Godwin, was a powerful advocate of political and social freedoms (including what was quaintly called "free love" —one can imagine his dismay when this particular belief came back to haunt him in the form of Mary's elopement with Shelley). Shelley, who had been expelled from Oxford (for writing a pamphlet called "The Necessity of Atheism"), enjoyed his position in the vanguard of the movement; and their friend Byron was notorious, both for his brilliance as a poet and his flamboyance as a political and social figure.

The sharp reader can find many Romantic themes in *Frankenstein*: the beauty and power of nature; the power of the supernatural; the appeal of the picturesque and exotic; the nobility of the common man; and especially, inherent goodness corrupted by "civilization." Other Romantics include philosophers such as Jean Jacques Rousseau, poets like Wordsworth, Coleridge, Schiller, and Blake, novelists like Dostoyevsky, Nathaniel Hawthorne, Sir Walter Scott and Victor Hugo, and composers like Beethoven, Schubert, Berlioz and Brahms.

In fact, the Shelleys weren't just casual neighbors of Lord Byron's. They were frequent visitors at the Villa Diodati, which Byron had rented—and so was Clare Clairmont, Mary's step-sister. Clare was an acknowledged part of the Shelley household during this period (as well as being Byron's mistress, and pregnant with his child), but she has vanished completely from Mary Shelley's 1831 account. At the time *Frankenstein* was first begun, the Shelleys were house guests at the lakeside villa. Also a part of the company was Byron's friend and personal physician, John Polidori.

The situation was explosive enough, with all those overactive libidos and artistic egos in one place at the same time…and then it started raining and it didn't let up. There wasn't even the possibility of long hikes across the landscape (the Romantic poets tended to be great walkers) to relieve the tedium. It was probably in a desperate attempt to keep people occupied that Lord Byron, the host, suggested that they all turn their hands to writing their own ghost stories.

Byron began a piece about the strange death of a gentleman traveling abroad, but he soon tired of it. It was published as "Fragment of a Novel" in the same volume as his *Mazeppa*. Polidori began what Mary Shelley described as

"some terrible idea about a skull-headed lady who was so punished for peeping through a key-hole—what to see I forget—something very shocking and wrong, of course." What he published in 1819, however, was "The Vampyre," a novella about Lord Ruthven, a nobleman who some critics have claimed is a highly unflattering portrait of Lord Byron himself. (Other critics have claimed that "The Vampyre" as a story bears a more-than-casual relationship to Byron's "Fragment.") Indeed, when "The Vampyre" was first published, anonymously, many people speculated that Byron had written it.)

"The Vampyre" may well have been the first vampire story written in English. But important as it is as a source and influence in the history of horror fiction, "The Vampyre" remains a seldom-read footnote in the history of literature. It was Mary Shelley who wrote what was to become a classic of horror and science fiction.

CHARACTERS

Victor Frankenstein. A student, first of alchemy, then of chemistry and natural philosophy; creator of the monster. He spends much of the book in the throes of remorse for what he has done, but his real sins are those of omission rather than

Prometheus

The subtitle of Frankenstein is "The Modern Prometheus." Mary Shelley, with the benefit of a classical education, counted on her readers to understand what she was saying with this subtitle. Modern readers less versed in Greek mythology may not get the reference at once. Prometheus was one of the Titans, a group of gods; with his brother Epimetheus (which means afterthought) Prometheus created the creatures of the Earth—including man. Because his enthusiastic brother had given away all the resources and qualities to lesser animals, Prometheus (*his* name means forethought) molded man from river clay, and daringly made him to walk upright. Prometheus then stole a torch of fire from the heavens and gave it to man, his favorite creation (apparently this was to make up, in part, for the strength, speed, and bravery—as well as the fur, fangs, feathers and scales—which his brother had given to lesser animals). The single gift of fire made man the superior of any other animal that walked the Earth.

But there was a price to pay. Prometheus's theft of fire had angered Zeus and the other Olympian gods (he'd also taught the humans to give the Gods only fat and bones from their animal sacrifices, and to keep the sirloin and chops for themselves). As a punishment, Zeus chained Prometheus to a rock high in the Caucasus Mountains, where an eagle came round every day to snack on his liver!

---

commission—he has left undone those things that he ought to have done, beginning with his failure to acknowledge and nurture the thing which he created.

All Victor's friends go on at length about what a wonderful and sensitive person he is. Even the monster speaks of him as "the select specimen of all that is worthy of love and admiration among men." But really, it's hard to see where all this enthusiasm comes from. Victor regularly neglects his family and friends in the pursuit of his studies, and his usual reaction to stress is to collapse in a fit of illness and delirium from which one or another of his friends or relatives has to come and rescue him. (In some ways Victor sounds a lot like Percy Bysshe Shelley, who lived off of money sent to him by Mary's father and took laudanum—a tincture of opium—for his nerves.)

William Frankenstein. Victor's much younger brother, killed by the monster after a brief, abortive attempt at friendly conversation. The boy, like almost everybody else, is repulsed by the monster and tries to run away, whereupon the monster strangles him.

Justine Moritz. A young girl in the Frankenstein household, in status somewhere between a maidservant and a foster daughter. The monster frames Justine for William's murder by leaving the boy's locket with her as she sleeps. Frankenstein knows what must have really happened, but while he is willing to protest Justine's innocence t

Frankenstein on Stage and Screen

Mary Shelley's story was soon adapted into dramatic form. The first stage version, *Frankenstein; or, the Man and the Monster*, appeared in 1823, and another—Richard Brinsley Peake's play, *Presumption; or, The Fate of Frankenstein*—appeared in the year of the book's second (1831) edition. The drama remained popular throughout the century, and when moving pictures were introduced it soon made the transition to film. There was a 1910 Thomas Alva Edison short film (of which almost nothing survives) showing the birth of the creature from a vat of chemicals, and a longer silent version in 1915.

It was the 1931 film version of *Frankenstein*, however, that sunk indelibly into the public consciousness. Such familiar bits as the hunchbacked assistant "Igor," the lonely castle, the accidentally obtained abnormal brain, are all elements from the film, not the original novel. "Boris Karloff" (born William Henry Pratt, and originally a chorister in musical comedies) was chosen for the part of the monster because of his height. The makeup developed for Karloff's version of the role created the modern image of the monster (as reflected in the Classics Illustrated comic as well): the high built-up forehead, the flat top to the head, the scars on the face and the bolts through the neck. The 1931 movie was followed by a number of sequels and spin-offs,

such as *Son of Frankenstein, Bride of Frankenstein*, and even *Jesse James Meets Frankenstein's Daughter*.

Over the years that followed, the story produced its own line of parody and humor: *Abbot and Costello Meet Frankenstein, Young Frankenstein*, Herman Munster in the TV series *The Munsters*, and (by way of the *New Yorker* cartoons of Charles Addams) the butler Lurch in *The Addams Family* TV series and movies. Possibly because of the popularity of the stage and film productions, the name "Frankenstein" eventually became attached not to the scientist, but to his creation. From there the term entered into American slang, where a "frankenstein" is a computer or other technical device put together out of parts from a variety of sources.

Mary Shelley's story saw other, later remakes in a serious vein, including at least three television versions in 1973, 1984, and 1993, as well as Kenneth Branagh's *Mary Shelley's Frankenstein* in 1994. In 1987, the director Ken Russell made *Gothic*—a film not about Victor Frankenstein and his monster, but about the events at the Villa Diodati at the time of the story's initial composition. The Russell movie was not particularly successful, however; nor did the later filmed versions of Mary Shelley's tale ever manage to achieve status as cultural icons in the way that Karloff's monster did.

the authorities, he stops short of explaining to them what he himself has done, and she is executed for a crime she did not commit.

Elizabeth Lavenza

Frankenstein's fiancée, an adopted child brought up with the family since her early youth. She's actually the daughter of an Italian revolutionary and his wife, originally left as a foster child with a Swiss peasant family.

Elizabeth is killed by the monster after Victor Frankenstein goes back on his promise to make the monster a female companion. The monster threatens Victor with the words "I will be with you on your wedding night," and Victor lacks the imagination to understand that *Elizabeth* is the one being threatened. He thinks that he will be the monster's chosen victim, but decides to go ahead and marry Elizabeth anyway. (It doesn't occur to Victor to tell Elizabeth about any of this. This is just one of the points at which it becomes difficult to sympathize with him wholeheartedly.) As usual, the miscalculation is Frankenstein's, but somebody else gets to pay for it.

Henry Clerval Frankenstein's best friend, who repeatedly comes to Victor's aid when he has worked himself into illness or depression. Clerval, like all of Frankenstein's other friends, is killed by the monster.

The Monster Frankenstein's creation. The monster has no name, and is, apparently, so ugly that everyone who sees him feels an instant revulsion. Victor Frankenstein describes him thus: *His yellow skin scarcely covered the work of muscles and arteries beneath; his hair was of a lustrous black, and flowing; his teeth of pearly whiteness; but these luxuriances only formed a more horrid contrast with his watery eyes, that seemed almost of the same color as the dun-white sockets in which they were set, his shriveled complexion and straight black lips.*

Despite this gruesome description, the monster is not evil from the moment of his "birth;" he becomes so after his preternatural ugliness causes even his maker to run from him in fear. Untaught, the creature's natural goodness (which is clearly shown in his account of his early, half-aware days and of his time spent in the unwitting company of the De Lacey family) remains stunted and undeveloped. When the monster's initial attempts at making human contact are met with violence and rejection, he takes this as the model for *his* subsequent behavior. With this, Victor Frankenstein's doom is sealed.

It's Alive!

You'll note, in reading the novel, that Victor Frankenstein does not go on record as saying "It's alive!" or anything else on beholding his creation. Raised as most of us are in a culture where the Frankenstein story is part of common lore, we tend to accept Victor Frankenstein's immediate rejection of the monster at its face value. Think a moment more, however, and you may wonder why it didn't occur to him that the thing would be horrific and loathesome *before* he gave it life; Frankenstein says "I had gazed on him while unfinished; he was ugly then, but when those muscles and joints were rendered capable of motion, it became a thing such as even Dante could not have conceived."

In fact, the monster sounds very like a newborn baby in some ways: it cannot control its body very well ("a convulsive motion agitated its limbs"), it makes incoherent noises ("His jaws opened, and he muttered some inarticulate sounds, while a grin wrinkled his cheeks. He might have spoken, but I did not hear"); he is wrinkled, inhumanly colored, and has a thick thatch of black hair. He's not a pretty baby and, unlike a normal human baby, there's not much hope that he's going to get better looking after the trauma of "birth" fades. Still, it's not hard to feel sorry for the creature, rejected by his "father" from the moment of his birth and left to fend for himself when he can barely walk.

Clearly Frankenstein did not build the monster because he was interested in parenting. So why does he? He tells us that "One of the phenomena which had peculiarly attracted my attention was the structure of the human frame, and, indeed, any animal endued with life. Whence, I often asked myself, did the principle of life proceed?" While that's a good question, it's a little passionless. In fact, adaptations of *Frankenstein* have dealt with Frankenstein's motives by making him somewhat unbalanced, or by giving him an incident in his past which explains his passion for playing around with the building blocks of life (in one recent film his mother's death drives him; in the novel, his mother's death is a cause for mourning, but not for creating life on the lab table).

In the end, Frankenstein's motives in making the monster seem slightly self-serving: "A new species would bless me as its creator and source; many happy and excellent natures would owe their being to me. No father could claim the gratitude of his child so completely as I should deserve theirs." Thinking that way, perhaps it's a little more understandable that his first impulse, on facing the reality of what he has done, is to run.

De Lacey The old blind man who lives, with his son **Felix** and his daughter **Agatha**, and their friend **Safie**, in a cottage in the woods. The monster's education comes from eavesdropping upon their lessons. Though he keeps himself hidden from them, he comes to feel an illusory sense of being part of their family group. When at last the monster nerves himself to speak with De Lacey, the young people burst in and—horrified by the monster's appearance—drive him away.

Old De Lacey is one of the "good parent" figures in the novel, along with Victor Frankenstein's own father and mother. Victor himself is a "bad parent," rejecting his creation—as, perhaps, William Godwin rejected young Mary after her mother's death (and, perhaps, as Percy Shelley abandoned the two children he'd had with Harriet).

Robert Walton The Arctic explorer who rescues Victor Frankenstein from the northern ice. Like so many of the other characters in the story, he has had an isolated, self-educated childhood. And like Frankenstein himself, he is ambitious and eager to win fame through the pursuit of scientific knowledge. He is, however, lonely: "I bitterly feel the want of a friend," he writes to his sister Margaret at the beginning of the book . What he gets, as it turns out, is Victor Frankenstein.

PLOT AND CONTEXT

Although the starting-point for Mary Shelley's tale was the image of the newly created monster coming to gaze upon his creator, the book became much more complex in its final structure. Shelley tells the story by means of three separate first-person narratives, embedded one within the other. The first narrative is the story told by the English explorer Robert Walton in letters to his sister. These letters begin and end the book, framing it, and deal with the events at the end of Victor Frankenstein's life. Within the letters we have the story which Frankenstein, after his rescue from the ice, tells to Walton. This narrative gives us the details of Frankenstein's early life, his creation and abandonment of the monster, and the monster's vengeful pursuit. Finally, at the center of the book, we have the monster's own recounting of what happened during the period between when he stumbled, barely aware of his own existence, out of Victor Frankenstein's labora-

tory, and when he confronted his creator after the death of young William Frankenstein. The monster's story is contained within Victor Frankenstein's narrative, which is contained in turn within Robert Walton's letters.

The Classics Illustrated adaptation of *Frankenstein* covers the main elements of the plot pretty thoroughly, although it leaves out the first part of Shelley's framing device, in which Arctic explorer Robert Walton discovers Victor Frankenstein, near the end of his search for the monster.

Victor Frankenstein leaves his home and family to study science at the University. While there, he becomes consumed with study, experimenting secretly with the very stuff of life itself. At last, his experiment is complete: he creates *life*, in the form of a monstrous creature. But as he looks on his creation Frankenstein's heart fails him: he rejects the monster, runs away, and suffers a breakdown. While he is recovering, he learns that his brother, little William, has been murdered, and that Justine Moritz, William's companion, is accused of the murder. When he returns home he finds the monster has preceded him—and is William's killer. Horrified, he hurries to protest Justine's innocence, although he stops short of telling who the real killer is. It doesn't matter, anyway: heartbroken and weary of the questioning, Justine confesses to the murder and is hanged.

Frankenstein confronts the monster, who tells him the tale of his long wandering after Frankenstein abandoned him. Driven from town to town, the monster finds a family living in the woods and "adopts" them, watching over them, learning to read, finally daring to speak to the old blind father. But the monster is discovered and driven away. Wandering again, he chances on young William, whom he kills accidentally; he implicates Justine in the murder by slipping William's locket in her pocket as she sleeps in the woods. His tale told, the monster begs Frankenstein to make him a companion, with whom he will leave for some remote land, leaving Victor untroubled. Frankenstein agrees—creates the monstrous "bride"—and in a moment of horror, destroys it.

Enraged, the monster swears "I will be with you on your wedding

BUT THE NEXT DARK DAWN FINDS JUSTINE PAYING THE WEIGHTY TOLL OF MURDER WITH HER OWN YOUNG LIFE.

I SHALL NEVER KNOW PEACE AGAIN. MAY THE ALMIGHTY HAVE MERCY ON THAT POOR INNOCENT GIRL'S SOUL.

BUT THE STRAIN OF FIENDISH LABOR SUDDENLY CAUSES VICTOR'S NERVES TO SNAP...

NO! NO! I CAN'T FINISH... I CAN'T!

The Lure of the Arctic

Mary Shelley frames her tale in the account of an Arctic adventure, and it is to the Arctic that the monster ultimately leads Frankenstein in what will become their mutual search for death. To understand these parts of the story, it's necessary to understand what the popular notion of the Arctic was in Mary Shelley's time.

The mid-18th century, in which *Frankenstein* is set, was a time of intense interest in Arctic exploration. Russian explorers like Vitus Bering ventured northward by sea, discovering such geographic landmarks as the Bering Straits and the Alaskan coast. (Shelley's fictional explorer, Robert Walton, also chooses the sea route out of the Russian port of Archangel.) English explorers, meanwhile, probed the interior of Canada north of

Hudson's Bay, until the French Revolution and the Napoleonic Wars put a temporary halt to exploratory voyages.

The Arctic (strictly speaking, the Antarctic) also figures in Samuel Taylor Coleridge's *Rime of the Ancient Mariner*, a poem with which Mary Shelley was well acquainted. At the age of nine, she was present when Coleridge read the poem aloud at her father's house, soon after its composi-

tion. There are deliberate references to the poem in Shelley's book, and the explorer Robert Walton quotes from it directly:

> *I am going to unexplored regions, to 'the land of mist and snow'; but I shall kill no albatross, therefore do not be alarmed for my safety, or if I should come back to you as worn and woeful as the Ancient Mariner. You will smile at my allusion; but I will disclose a secret. I have often attributed my attachment to, my passionate enthusiasm for, the dangerous mysteries of the ocean, to that production of the most imaginative of modern poets.*

Shelley is, perhaps, speaking as much for herself as for Robert Walton. She sends out her fictional explorer into a region which promises both profit and scientific enlightenment: profit in the search for the northwest passage (a direct sea route to the Pacific that would make unnecessary the long voyages around the Horn and the Cape of Good Hope) and enlightenment in the quest for "the secret of the magnet." More than that, though, at the start of his journey Walton believes that the Arctic will prove to be "a region of beauty and delight":

> There, Margaret, the sun is
> forever visible, its broad disk
> just skirting the horizon, and
> diffusing a perpetual splen-
> dour. There—for with your
> leave, my sister, I will put
> some trust in preceding nav-
> igators—there frost and
> snow are banished; and,
> sailing over a calm sea, we
> may be wafted to a land sur-
> passing in wonders and in
> heavenly beauty every region
> hitherto discovered on the
> habitable globe. Its produc-
> tions and features may be
> without example, as the phe-
> nomena of the heavenly bod-
> ies undoubtedly are in those
> undiscovered solitudes. What
> may not be expected in a
> country of eternal light?

In fact, the Arctic is not a country of perpetual light. Half of the far northern year is spent in darkness, something which Robert Walton should have known if he had, as he says, sailed in the Greenland whale fishery. Whether Mary Shelley was herself unaware of this fact is hard to say, but— given that she was an educated woman, the daughter and the associate of intellectuals who were themselves well-read in science and natural philosophy—such ignorance is unlikely. What *is* likely is that she is exaggerating Walton's ideal- istic conception of the north into a one-sided vision of pure good, the better to disillusion him later.

night!" Fleeing the monster's rage, Frankenstein finds himself accused of the murder of his best friend, Henry Clerval, and breaks down again, certain that the monster was the murderer. He is cleared, returns

ALAS! WHAT IS THIS DREADFUL APPREHENSION I FEEL, CLOUDING THE HAPPIEST DAY OF MY LIFE...

home to recuperate, and decides at last to marry his patient fiancée, Elizabeth. But the monster's specter hangs over the wedding: he is indeed with them on their wedding night, and kills Elizabeth. Now it is Frankenstein who pursues the mon- ster, all the way to the Arctic—and the story comes full circle, with Frankenstein finishing his story to explorer Robert Walton. Frankenstein's death leaves the mon- ster without purpose; consumed with grief at his maker's death, he seeks his own death.

The Science in FRANKENSTEIN

Mary Shelley is never specific about the actual means by which Victor Frankenstein brings his creation to life— she employs the technique, used to good effect by science fiction writers ever since, of artful vagueness about those

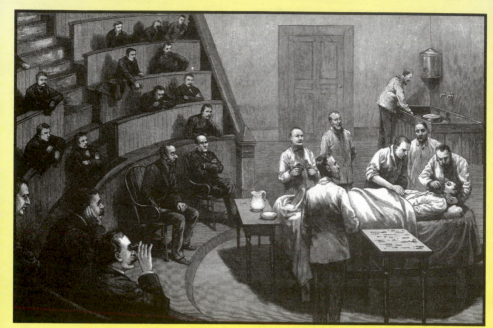

processes which go beyond the actual known science of the day. "I see by your eagerness and the wonder and hope which your eyes express, my friend, that you expect to be informed of the secret with which I am acquainted," Frankenstein says to his rescuer; "that cannot be: listen patiently until the end of my story, and you will easily perceive why I am reserved upon that subject."

However, the members of the house party at the Villa Diodati were an educated lot, acquainted with the scientific theories of the day. The physician Polidori, for example, had been the youngest person ever to graduate from the University of Edinburgh medical school. When they weren't reading ghost stories aloud (including "The Golem," by Gustav Meyrink, about an artificial being created from clay), Mary Shelley reports that "...various philosophical doctrines were discussed, and among others the nature of the principle of life, and whether there was any probability of its being discovered and communicated.... Perhaps a corpse would be re-animated; galvanism had given token of such things: perhaps the component parts of a creature might be manufactured, brought together, and endued with vital warmth."

The "galvanism" which Mary Shelley speaks of refers to the famous experiments performed in the 1780s by an Italian professor of anatomy named Luigi Galvani, who discovered that the leg muscles of a dissected frog would twitch when electric current passed through them. Galvani initially attributed the contraction to an intrinsic quality in the leg muscles, which he referred to as "animal electricity." By the end of the century another Italian, the physicist Alessandro Volta, had determined the true source of the electric current—two dissimilar metals, plus moisture (in the case of Galvani's experiment, the brass hooks on which the frog hung from an iron trellis, and the moist tissue of the frog's legs).

Percy Shelley himself had experimented with electricity and galvanism while he was at Oxford. His friend James Hogg later described these experiments:

> [He] proceeded with much eagerness and enthusiasm, to show me the various instruments, especially the electrical apparatus; turning round the handle very rapidly, so that the fierce, crackling sparks flew forth; and presently standing on the stool with glass feet, he begged me to work the machine until he was filled with fluid [electricity], so that his long, wild locks bristled and stood on end ....

If Percy Shelley's university experiments provided some of the scientific background for Mary's story, his headlong enthusiasm may well have given her a model for Victor Frankenstein in his early days as a researcher.

Of as much interest to Shelley's audience—and of vital importance to the horrific-ness of the story—is the question of where Frankenstein got the spare

ENDLESS WEEKS PASS... EACH DAY FINDING VICTOR MORE INTENSE AT HIS STUDY AND WORK...

IF I COULD ONLY FIND THE KEY TO BANISH DISEASE FROM THE HUMAN FRAME AND RENDER MAN INVULNERABLE TO ANY BUT A VIOLENT DEATH. IF... IF! AND I COME SO CLOSE.

parts to build his creature:

> I collected bones from charnel-houses and disturbed, with profane fingers, the tremendous secrets of the human frame. In a solitary chamber, or rather cell, at the top of the house, and separated from all the other apartments by a gallery and staircase, I kept my workshop of filthy creation; my eyeballs were starting from their sockets in attending to the details of my employment. The dissecting room and the slaughter-house furnished many of my materials; and often did my human nature turn with loathing from my occupation, whilst, still urged on by an eagerness which perpetually increased, I brought my work near to a conclusion.

As gruesome as this sounds, it wasn't unusual. The only way researchers and surgeons in Shelley's time were able to learn about human anatomy was by using the bodies of criminals who had been executed, or by illegally obtaining bodies—body-snatching. Some surgeons hired "resurrection men," who dug up freshly buried bodies almost as soon as the last shovel of earth had been thrown over them. Curiously enough, a

Style: Building Blocks of Horror

How does *Frankenstein* scare the reader? Modern readers may think they know the story too well to be really scared by it. But the novel still manages to raise hairs on the back of a reader's neck. How?

By contrast: in the months before the monster's "birth," Frankenstein tells us "It was a most beautiful season; never did the fields bestow a more plentiful harvest or the vines yield a more luxurient vintage." But, he adds, he sees none of it, totally absorbed in his researches. When the monster fulfills its vow and joins Frankenstein on his wedding night, the man goes from his greatest joy to his greatest grief, all in a moment's space.

With language: Shelley doesn't get very graphic, but her descriptions—both of physical scenes and of states of mind—are powerful. Consider the moment when Frankenstein finds the monster with Elizabeth:

> *Great God! Why did I not then expire? Why am I here to relate the destruction of the best hope and the purest creature on earth? She was there, lifeless and inanimate, thrown across the bed, her head hanging down and her pale and distorted features half covered by her hair. Everywhere I turn I see the same figure—her bloodless arms and relaxed form flung by the murderer on its bridal bier. Could I behold this and live?*

With foreshadowing: after the monster is born, Frankenstein has a dream of Elizabeth from which the monster wakes him:

> *…but as I imprinted the first kiss on her lips, they became livid with the hue of death; her features appeared to change, and I thought I held the corpse of my dead mother in my arms; a shroud enveloped her form, and I saw the grave-worms crawling in the folds of the flannel. I started from my sleep with horror; a cold dew covered my forehead, my teeth chattered, and every limb became convulsed; when, by the dim and yellow light of the moon, as it forced its way through the window shutters, I beheld the wretch—the miserable monster I had created.*

Much later in the book, on Frankenstein's wedding night, the monster again wakens him from a kind of dream—the dream of living a normal life. The earlier image sets up a reader's expectation that *something* is bound to happen—and when Shelley delivers, the impact is that much more powerful.

You can still find current day writers, and film makers, using the same tricks to give a reader (or viewer) that prickly sense of expectation and dread that a satisfying horror story evokes in all of us.

corpses delivered by Burke and Hare, was never prosecuted for receiving the bodies.

The Genre of FRANKENSTEIN

Mary Shelley's work is not a realistic novel of the sort that, by 1816, had already been written in England for more than a century by the likes of Daniel Defoe, Henry Fielding, and Jane Austen. In form, it is similar to the philosophical romances of Voltaire (of which *Candide* is likely the most famous). *Frankenstein* is also related to the Gothic novels which had enjoyed a vogue during the 18th century, lurid tales of the supernatural with titles like *The Monk, The Castle of Otranto,* or *Melmoth the Wanderer.*

In some ways, *Frankenstein* is a precursor of the science fiction genre, as the form would develop a century or so later. You can find many of the characteristics of twentieth century science fiction in *Frankenstein* in embryonic form: the use of imagined advancements in contemporary scientific knowledge (in this case, new developments in the fields of electricity and anatomy); the emphasis on "pushing the envelope" both in exploration and in scientific experimentation; and a concern with the moral issues raised by scientific development, as well as with the effect of science on the people of the story.

Frankenstein is also among the literary ancestors of the modern horror story. Mary Shelley herself said of her intentions, "I busied myself *to think of a*

-erson got into very little trouble for aving an unexplained corpse hanging bout—so long as there were no grave-lothes on the body when it was found; f there were graveclothes, the punish-ent was seven years' transportation. nd even body-snatching wasn't the vorst of it; in the 1820s two enterprising rave-robbers, William Burke and Villiam Hare, took to serial murder in rder to keep up with the demand for adavers. When the murder of their 16th ictim led to their capture, Hare turned Crown's evidence; Burke was hanged in 829. Significantly, Robert Knox, the octor who had bought most of the

HOW WELL I RECALL FATHER EXPLAINING THE ELEMENTS OF ELECTRICITY TO ME WHEN I WAS A CHILD. ITS POWER FOR DESTRUCTION FILLS ME WITH AWE.

story,—a story to rival those which had excited us to this task. One which would speak to the mysterious fears of our nature and awaken thrilling horror—one to make the reader dread to look round, to curdle the blood, and quicken the beatings of the heart."

This concern for the production of a specific emotional reaction—usually terror, horror, revulsion—is characteristic of the horror tale. The genre continued its development during the 19th century through the works of Edgar Allen Poe (among others), and arrived in the modern era with some of its effects and monsters altered but with its essential goals intact.

THEMES: Monsters and Over-reachers

One of the sources for the novel was the figure Prometheus, from the classic legend. All the Romantics knew the story of the immortal who stole fire from the gods to benefit humanity, and who was punished for his presumption.

The poets, Percy Shelley especially, identified with the heroic figure of the god-defying Prometheus; Mary, though, looked at the story from a different angle. Mary Shelley's Promethean figure, Victor Frankenstein, is not especially heroic. He fails to realize that his act of knowledge-stealing defiance may have consequences, or that he may have a responsibility toward what he has created.

By the time Frankenstein admits his own responsibility for the monster's actions, it's too late for him to do anything except try to kill it. He never does understand the point that the monster is trying to force him to accept—that his most grievous crime was not the making of the monster. It was his refusal to acknowledge the creature as his own (if unnaturally produced) offspring, and to nurture the goodness which it quite clearly possesses and has the power to recognize.

Outside of the world of myth and

SON, YOU'VE GOT TO THINK OF OTHER THINGS BESIDES THE WONDERS OF STEAM AND ELECTRICITY. SCIENCE HAS ITS PLACE, BUT A MAN MUST THINK OF A WIFE, TOO, YOU KNOW!

UNTIL I SATISFY MY THIRST FOR KNOWLEDGE IN CHEMISTRY, I SHALL FEEL UNWORTHY OF ELIZABETH. SHE UNDERSTANDS.

legend, one of the great overreachers of the early 19th century was Napoleon Bonaparte, who in the aftermath of the French Revolution rose from an army corporal to make himself Emperor of France. The French Revolution itself began as a revolt against tyranny, but it led first to the Reign of Terror and then to Napoleon's attempted conquest of all Europe. Mary Shelley grew up in a household of English intellectuals who had supported the revolution in its early stages, and in a country which had been at war with revolutionary and imperial France for most of her life. Napoleon's ultimate fall at the Battle of Waterloo had taken place only a year before the summer house-party during which Shelley's book was begun. Napoleon's dramatic career, and the Revolution which preceded it, would have provided Shelley with a real-life example of how noble aims and high ambitions can result in dreadful consequences.

A less dire figure, but one closer to home, may have been Mary's own husband, Percy Bysshe Shelley: radical, atheist, sponger off his father-in-law, unfaithful husband, and undeniably great poet.

And finally, we should not ignore Mary Shelley herself. Her birth killed her mother, and by the time *Frankenstein* had finished evolving into its first published form, her elopement with Shelley had—in a sense—killed the poet's first wife, Harriet. Mary's half-sister, Fanny Imlay, killed herself during this period, leaving behind a letter whose words seem an eerie echo of the monster's desolation: "I have long determined that the best thing I could do was put an end to the existence of a being whose birth was unfortunate, and whose life has only been a series of pain to those persons who have hurt their health in endeavouring to promote her welfare. Perhaps to hear of my death will give you pain, but you will soon have the blessing of forgetting that such a creature existed as...(*Fanny*)"

Mary had dared a great deal, choosing to leave her home and family and defy the conventions of her day for the sake of her life with Percy Shelley. But her act of defiance did not come without cost, both to Mary herself and to those others who were affected by her actions. Her awareness of this cost pervades the story, and colors both the remorse of Victor Frankenstein and the vengeful anger of his lonely, unloved creation.

STUDY QUESTIONS

• Why might Mary Shelley have chosen the threefold story-within-a-story structure for *Frankenstein*? What is gained (or lost) by having three distinct first-person narrators? Do you find the central section, told by the monster, to be more or less frightening than the surrounding parts? Why?

• One of the Monster's victims is Victor Frankenstein's your brother William. Do you think it's significant that Mary Shelley's father was named William? What about the fact that she also gave that name to the son who was born during the time between 1816 and 1818 when she was working on putting *Frankenstein* into final form?

• All the women in the Frankenstein household have been adopted or rescued in some manner—Victor's mother was saved from poverty by her (much older) husband, Elizabeth was adopted, and Justine was given employment as a form of shelter from the dislike of her own mother. None of them were "born into" the family

I DECIDED TO TAKE HIM WITH ME AND TEACH HIM TO BE MY FRIEND. EVERY MAN NEEDS A FRIEND...

NO! NO! PUT ME DOWN!

HUSH, LITTLE MAN. I WON'T HURT YOU...

Frankenstein and his creation might have led to this contradictory reaction?

• Does the barren Arctic waste with its extreme cold symbolize emotional or moral emptiness in the main characters of *Frankenstein*?

• From the moment when Victor Frankenstein rejects his creature, it seems that an unhappy ending is inevitable. But imagine that, instead of abandoning the monster, Frankenstein had stayed with, and nurtured, his creature. What problems would he have faced? How would the ending have changed? Is a happy ending possible for Frankenstein?

as Victor and William were. What do you think is the significance of this, in terms of the themes of the story? How does this idea relate to the larger ideas of family and responsibility, and how does it contrast with Victor's treatment of the monster?

TOO LATE... A WIDENING GULF BREACHED SHIP AND ICE...

LOOK, CAPTAIN! HE'S FLOATING NORTH, HE'LL PERISH!

'TIS BETTER THIS WAY, HE IS A MONSTER, POLLUTED BY BITTER CRIMES AND TORN BY REMORSE. DEATH TO HIM!

"He was soon borne away by the waves, and lost in the darkness and distance."

• The monster claims to hate Frankenstein, and has certainly done him many injuries, all the way to causing the deaths of his family and friends. Yet the explorer Robert Walton reports that upon Frankenstein's death the monster is overcome by grief, and intends to commit suicide: "I shall collect my funeral pile," the monster says, "and consume to ashes this miserable frame .... I shall die, and what I now feel will no longer be felt." What aspects of the relationship between Victor

About the Essayist:

Debra Doyle holds a Ph.D from the University of Pennsylvania, and has taught at Penn, Villanova, and the University of New Hampshire.

With her husband James Macdonald, Dr. Doyle is the author of adult and young adult fantasy and science fiction, including the popular Mageworld series.